#4 Ant Attack

Books in the
S.W.I.T.C.H. series

S.W.I.T.C.H.

#4 Ant Attack

Ali Sparkes

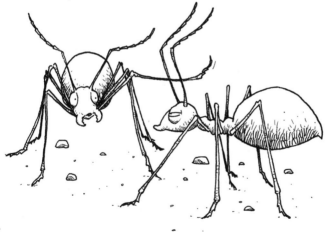

illustrated by
Ross Collins

MINNEAPOLIS

Text © Ali Sparkes 2011
Illustrations © Ross Collins 2011

"SWITCH: Ant Attack" was originally published in English in 2011. This
edition is published by an arrangement with Oxford University Press.

Copyright © 2013 by Darby Creek

Darby Creek
A division of Lerner Publishing Group, Inc.
241 First Avenue North
Minneapolis, MN 55401 U.S.A.

Website address: www.lernerbooks.com

Main body text set in ITC Goudy Sans Std. 14/19.
Typeface provided by Monotype Typography.

Library of Congress Cataloging-in-Publication Data

Sparkes, Ali.
        Ant attack / by Ali Sparkes ; illustrated by Ross Collins.
           p.   cm. — (S.W.I.T.C.H. ; #04)
        Summary: During an unwelcome visit, neighbor Tarquin unwittingly uses
   SWITCH spray to turn twins Josh and Danny into ants, then sets out with a
   magnifying glass to fry some bugs.
        ISBN 978-0-7613-9202-6 (lib. bdg. : alk. paper)
        [1. Ants—Fiction. 2. Brothers—Fiction. 3. Twins—Fiction. 4. Science
   fiction.] I. Collins, Ross, ill. II. Title.
   PZ7.S73712Ant 2013
   [Fic]—dc23   2012026635

Manufactured in the United States of America
1 – SB – 12/31/12

For Katie Ann

Danny and Josh
(and Piddle)

They may be twins, but they're NOT the same! Josh loves insects, spiders, beetles, and bugs. Danny can't stand them. Anything little with multiple legs freaks him out. So sharing a bedroom with Josh can be . . . erm . . . interesting. Mind you, they both love putting earwigs in big sister Jenny's underwear drawer . . .

Danny
- FULL NAME: Danny Phillips
- AGE: eight years
- HEIGHT: taller than Josh
- FAVORITE THING: skateboarding
- WORST THING: creepy-crawlies and cleaning
- AMBITION: to be a stuntman

Josh

- FULL NAME: Josh Phillips
- AGE: eight years
- HEIGHT: taller than Danny
- FAVORITE THING: collecting insects
- WORST THING: skateboarding
- AMBITION: to be an entomologist

Piddle

- FULL NAME: Piddle the dog Phillips
- AGE: two dog years (fourteen in human years)
- HEIGHT: not very
- FAVORITE THING: chasing sticks
- WORST THING: cats
- AMBITION: to bite a squirrel

Contents

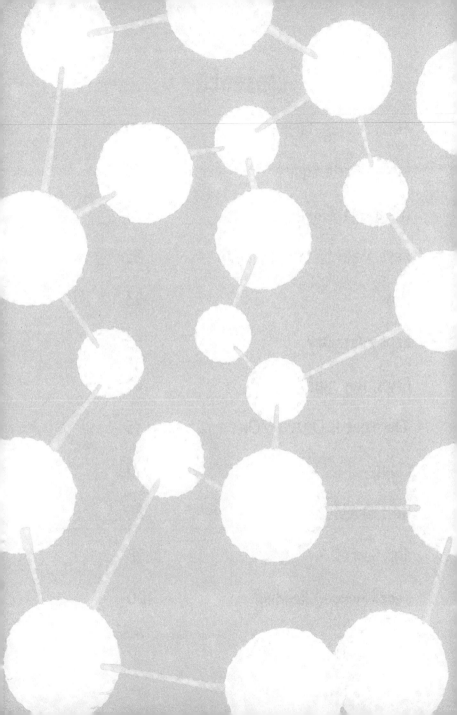

Entertaining Tarquin

"Guess what, boys?" Mom peered around the bedroom door with a grin.

Josh and Danny paused in their fight with rolled-up newspaper swords. They smiled innocently at her.

"What?" urged Danny.

The grin got stiffer. "Tarquin's here to play!" Mom gulped. The looks on her twin sons' faces were dark. It felt as if Halloween had arrived early.

"*Tarquin*," said Josh.

"Here," said Danny.

Piddle the dog whined and shot under the bunk bed.

Danny threw down his sword. He turned to Josh and opened out his arms. He commanded:

"Through the heart. And make it quick."

"Oh, come on! It'll be *fun*!" said Mom. "Sshhh! He's coming up the stairs."

They could clearly hear Tarquin approaching. He appeared to be singing opera.

"But we can't *stand* Tarquin!" hissed Danny, pushing his messy blond hair off his furrowed forehead. "And you don't even *like* his mom! Remember how snotty she was about you winning the best garden contest?"

Mom sighed. She said in a low voice, "I've let bygones be bygones! His mom needed help today. She's visiting a sick aunt. We have to look after each other. We're a *community*! Oh—here he is now!"

Tarquin trailed past her into Josh and Danny's room. At seven and a half, he was nearly their age, but he looked about fifty-five. He was dressed in neatly ironed pants, a blue shirt, and a proper matching jacket. His hair was severely parted and combed flat to his head. His googly gray eyes narrowed as he examined their room. "It's rather a mess, isn't it?" he said, in his peculiar high-pitched voice.

"Well, duh!" said Danny. "It's a boys' room!"

"Yes," said Tarquin. "And so is mine. But I still refrain from growing fungus in it." He eyed a jar of something gooey on the windowsill. The jar had once been filled with tadpoles. Josh had set them free in the garden pond last week. It *had* gotten a little furry.

"Have fun, boys," called Mom, already halfway downstairs.

Tarquin began to wander around, poking at their stuff. He prodded their comics and sniffed. "*So* childish."

Danny mouthed, "*Childish? Spider-Man?*" at Josh and picked up his sword again. Josh frowned at him and shook his head.

"So what do you read then, Tarquin?" said Josh, trying hard to sound friendly.

"Oh—*Classical Music* magazine. *New Scientist*. You wouldn't know them. I don't suppose you know anything about the arts or science."

"We know a *lot* about science!" burst out Danny. "We've had more science in the last six weeks than you've had in your life, you little—"

"Shut up, Danny," said Josh. He was worried about what his brother might say next. Maybe he would tell Tarquin that he and Josh had been involved with scientific experiments. They were so amazing that every scientist in the world would explode with astonishment if they knew. Maybe he'd boast that they'd been turned into spiders, then flies, and then grasshoppers over this year. This was after getting tangled up with the brilliant (but quite probably crazy) old lady scientist next door.

Petty Potts seemed like a dotty old dear, but she

was in fact a genius. She had created S.W.I.T.C.H. spray, which could turn any creature into a creepy-crawly. She'd made a drinkable version too, and that was even stronger. What's more, if Josh and Danny managed to help her find the missing parts of her REPTOSWITCH formula, she could change them into alligators or giant pythons! It was a fantastic secret. Josh was determined that Danny wouldn't blurt it out to Tarquin.

"Oh—don't be offended," Tarquin was saying now. He picked up Josh's magnifying glass from the top of their bookcase and turned it over in one hand. "My mother says you can't help it that you're not as clever as me. It's not your fault."

THWACK! Danny brought down his sword. He aimed for the back of Tarquin's neatly combed head. But Josh caught it with an upswing of his own sword. "*Stop it!*" he mouthed at Danny. Tarquin put down the magnifying glass and moved on.

"We *do* know quite a lot about science—especially nature," said Josh. "We know about creepy-crawlies. Let's take my magnifying glass outside. I'll show you some in the yard if you like."

Tarquin shuddered. "Ugh! If you show me a creepy-crawly, I'll stamp on it."

Josh was shocked. He was a great nature lover. He had adored all kinds of creepy-crawlies long before he'd ever been one. Even Danny, who wasn't fond of them at all, would never deliberately squash one.

"You can't *step* on them! That's just stupid!"

"No—sometimes I look at them first," smirked Tarquin. "It's quite fun to pull their legs off."

"It's not fun for *them*!" said Josh, feeling quite hot in the face. He picked up his sword, ready to swing it into Tarquin's head. But this time, Danny grabbed it, raised his eyebrows, and waggled his finger at his brother.

Tarquin opened the door to their toy cupboard. Then he screamed.

Nasty Little Squirt

Danny and Josh knew to hop quickly out of the way whenever they opened the toy cupboard door. Tarquin was not trained to handle the danger. The avalanche that engulfed him took him completely by surprise.

He squealed loudly. He struggled to sit up in a river of games, books, Legos, blocks, old stuffed animals, trading cards, *Thunderbirds* aircraft, *Thomas the Tank Engine* characters and bits of railroad, assorted guns and light sabers, action figures, and remote control cars. And quite a few cheesy socks. "I'LL GET YOU!" warned the talking Action Man.

"Oops! Toy quake!" said Josh, with a delighted smile. The toy cupboard had done exactly what he and Danny had been longing to do. It had smacked Tarquin off his feet and wiped the smug look off his face.

A couple of water pistols bounced out, and Danny picked them up. "Come on," he said. "Let's go and play with these outside." He and Josh ran downstairs without waiting to see if Tarquin was following. They shot through the front door. They ran around the side of the house to fill up their water pistols from the outside faucet.

"Ah! Josh! Danny!" said a voice above them.

They looked up to see Petty Potts leaning over the low brick wall. It separated their two houses. She clutched a large net on a pole. "How are you both since last week's adventure? Any aftereffects?" She glanced around shiftily. Then she peered closely at them through her dusty spectacles.

"We're fine," said Josh, putting the stopper into his filled-up water pistol. "Danny's not rubbing his legs together anymore. We've both stopped spitting out brown goo and jumping all over the room when we get nervous."

"Good, good," smiled Petty, placing a spray bottle on the wall. "I was a bit concerned. But you were *splendid* grasshoppers, I have to say! Still on the lookout for the REPTOSWITCH cubes too, are you? Haven't given up the search, I hope."

"We're always on the lookout, you know that," said Josh.

Danny looked warily at the spray bottle. "What's *that?*" he asked.

"Oh—another S.W.I.T.C.H. spray. Very fast acting. Going to try it on some ducks in the pond at the park," said Petty, airily. She tugged at the net. "I haven't S.W.I.T.C.H.ed any birds yet. I need a nice strong squirty jet to reach them before they fly off."

"You should be careful!" warned Josh. "One day someone's going to catch you doing it!"

"One day, everyone *will* know about my work!" said Petty. She puffed her chest out and patted her wavy gray hair. "I will have a grand exhibition as soon as it's perfected. After we've found the last three REPTOSWITCH cubes to add to the BUGSWITCH cubes, of course. It'll be much more impressive than you two morphing into grasshoppers. Don't forget, you'll be able to try out being an alligator or an anaconda!" She wiggled her eyebrows for effect, like a rather creepy children's entertainer. "But for now, it has to stay our secret."

"Joshua! Daniel! Where are you?" came a shrill voice. Uh-oh. Tarquin was in the front yard, looking for them. "Come *out*, you oafs! If I *have* to join in your stupid game, I want a water pistol too! Get *me* one, or I'll tell your mother you're being mean to me!"

Josh and Danny ran down the side passage and into the backyard, giggling.

Petty Potts stared after them for a moment. Then she noticed a large pigeon on her driveway. "Hmmm . . . you might do," she murmured. She edged toward it with her net. Needing both hands free, she left the spray bottle on the wall.

Josh and Danny were ready with the water pistols as Tarquin came trotting around the side of the house into the backyard. As soon as he came into view, they let him have both barrels.

"Ooooh! Ooooh! That's not fair!" he whined. Then he ran toward them and squirted them both back.

"Where did you get the water pistol?" spluttered Josh. He wiped away drips from his face, grinning. He was glad that Tarquin was at least joining in.

"It's not a pistol," sniffed Tarquin. "You didn't give me one, did you? But I got you both back anyway! I just used this spray bottle I found on the wall."

Josh and Danny stared, aghast, at the bottle in Tarquin's hand. Then at each other.

Tarquin, rubbing water out of his eyes, heard Josh wail, "Oh *no*—not *again*!" But when he opened his eyes, both twins had vanished.

It's a Girl Thing

"Oh great. Just great," said Josh. He lay on his back at the bottom of a deep, dark chasm. He did a quick leg count.

"How many legs this time?" wailed a fearful voice behind him. "Please don't say it's eight. Please don't say it's eight. Please d—"

"Six! It's six!" called back Josh. "Relax."

Danny scrambled to his six feet. He looked around the shadowy gorge they had fallen into when they shrank to creepy-crawly size. Again. "Where are we?" he whispered. His voice echoed back quickly off the rocky walls on either side of him.

"And what are we?"

"I reckon we're down in a crack in the sidewalk," said Josh. "So we must be pretty small." He turned around to peer at his brother. They both gave a little shout of shock.

"Eeeww!"

Each brother was staring at a glossy dark-brown head with small round black eyes and long twitching feelers. Their almost-black bodies were sleek and shiny. They were made up of three parts: a big oval head with small pincerlike jaws; a little bottle-shaped bit in the middle, from which their six muscular but elegant legs sprouted; and the biggest bit at the back, which tapered off into what looked like a stinger.

"Wow! We're ants!" breathed Josh. A rich scent wafted around him.

"Could be worse," gulped Danny. He didn't much like any creepy-crawlies but definitely coped better with the little six-legged ones.

"This is amazing," marveled Josh. "I mean . . . we're talking—right?"

"Well, obviously," said Danny. He shrugged and turned his feelers up like the palms of his hands.

"But we're not making any noise!"

"Don't be stupid! I can hear you," said Danny.

"No! You only think you can hear me. But I'm actually not talking out loud! Ants can't do that. They talk to each other by making smells and prodding with their feelers!" squeaked Josh, excitedly. He prodded Danny with his feelers.

"OK," said Danny. "So—I'm not hearing a word you say . . . ? I'm just smelling them."

"And feeling them!" added Josh with another prod.

"All right," said Danny, prodding Josh back sharply. "I get it. But all this sniffy, poky chatting isn't getting us anywhere. We're tiny insects—again! And you know that every time we turn into tiny insects, something tries to eat us." He looked fearfully up and down the narrow dark gorge. It seemed to be deserted.

"I'll tell you what else is weird!" said Josh. He turned around in a circle, looking back down his new body.

"What?" said Danny. "What could possibly be more weird than turning into an ant?"

"Well . . . um . . ." Josh stared at Danny. His feelers shuddered. "We're not just ants. We've changed a little bit more than that."

"What are you talking about?" Danny poked Josh between the eyes with one feeler. "Get to the point before something decides we're its mid-morning snack!"

"We're girls."

Danny staggered backward. "We're what?"

"You heard me. We're not boys now. We're girls. Check it out!" He pointed over his shoulder with his front right leg. "No wings!"

"But we're ants! Not flies."

"Ah—but if we were boy ants, we'd have wings. All the other ants are girls. Even soldier ants are girls."

"Oh great," muttered Danny. He peered back over his own shoulder now. "Are you sure? I mean, couldn't there be wings tucked inside somewhere?"

"Nah—that's beetles. Face it, Dan, we're ants and we're girl ants."

"I'm never going to forgive Petty Potts for this!" Danny spat. "And if you ever tell anyone . . ."

He stopped dead, suddenly picking up a vibrating sensation. Josh was looking scared.

"What's that?" he whispered.

He and Danny peered along the narrow chasm. They could feel warm air blowing against their feelers. There was a strong smell. To Danny, it was a bit like the time when they'd gone on the subway. While waiting in the station, they'd noticed the weird warm wind coming out of the tunnel just before the train hurtled through.

"Something's coming!" squeaked Josh. "Something fast and big!"

The vibrations seemed deafening—even if they couldn't actually hear them. The smell was very strong. Danny scrambled up the wall into a small alcove. He reached down and grabbed Josh's head with his strong jaws.

"WHOO-AAH!" shrieked Josh. His legs flapped wildly as something hurtled along toward him like a runaway train. "It's going to hit me! It's going to hit me!" Then his screams were abruptly stopped.

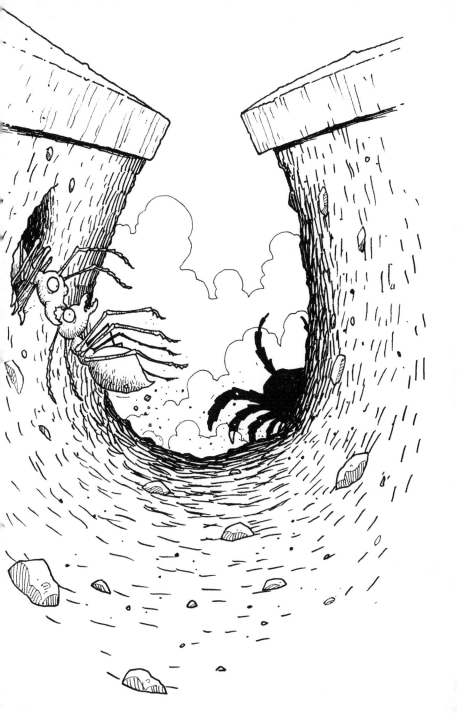

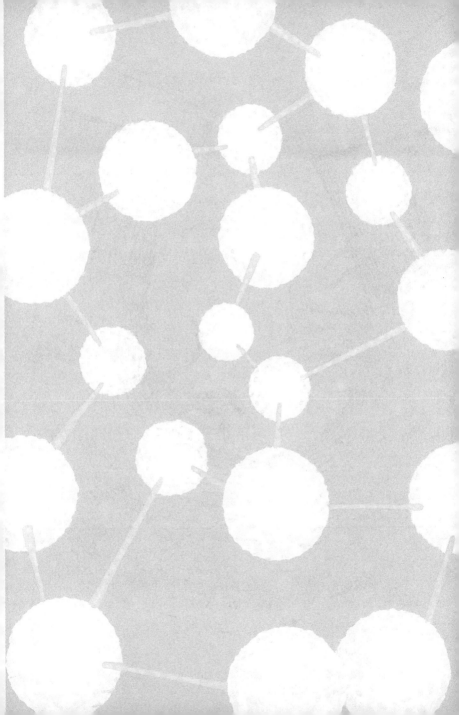

Fast Train to Munchville

Josh's breath was bashed out of him as he flipped up and over. Below him the thundering got even more intense and there was a blur of red. He found himself suddenly upsidedown next to Danny, who was still biting his brother's head. Danny was scared to let go as the air around them rushed along and tried to suck them out of their alcove.

"It's a train! A subway train!" squawked Josh, even though he knew it couldn't be.

"No—it's something worse," said Danny. "Subway trains don't ever try to eat you. But I bet that would!"

"Danny! O-ow! Do you mind?" said Josh. Danny at last un-bit him. Josh looked down to see the blur of red slowing down. Now he could make out legs. Lots of legs, on either side of a long, glistening segmented body. "It's a centipede!" he whispered.

"Looks like a millipede to me!" replied Danny. "All those legs!"

"I wish it was," groaned Josh. "Millipedes are vegetarians. But that's a centipede all right. You can tell by the way its legs are quite long and its body is in segments. And the long leggy things at the back." As he said this, the long leggy things swept past below them. Josh heaved a sigh of relief.

Then he sucked it all back in again as the centipede slowed to a halt. Its long back legs were twitching and then, slowly, began to creep backward.

"Oh no," groaned Danny. "This is not good. This is so not good! Do they—do they eat ants?"

"Yep," gulped Josh. "They're the most incredible hunters. They've got poison fangs. They go for anything that moves—even each other."

The red train below them was still backing up. Leg after leg rippled backward. Then a reddish-brown face suddenly lurched up at them, its fangs quivering. Danny and Josh didn't wait to say hello.

Instinctively they swung around and shot
something out of their abdomens into the
centipede's face. The creature flinched backward
with an angry grunt. Then they took off along the
wall as fast at their six legs would carry them.

"GO! GO! GO! GO!" squeaked Danny. Josh's
berry-shaped backside scooted along in front of
him. It took him several seconds to realize that he
and Josh were both running sideways, along the
wall.

He also realized that the centipede wasn't
chasing them. "Hey! Hey, Josh!" he shouted—

although he knew it wasn't really a shout at all, just a waft of some kind of whiffy chemical. "We got away! We did it!"

Josh turned around on the wall and stared back along the gorge. It was true. The centipede was gone. "Ha!" said Josh. "He didn't much like a bit of acid in the face!"

"What—you mean we just kind of peed acid?" Danny waggled his feelers excitedly. They reached a corner where some sunlight shafted in and a clump of large furry green leaves with some heavy bell-shaped purple flowers grew. "How cool is that? Killer pee!"

"Formic acid," said Josh. "Look—see what happens when I do this." He aimed his backside at one of the flowers and squirted out some more. The petals shook as the jet of liquid hit them. Then they began to change color—from purple to pink to a paler pink. "See," said Josh. "It makes them change color. Acid. Ant defense!"

Danny clapped his feelers together. "Ants are brilliant!" he giggled. Then he remembered he was a girl. He stopped giggling.

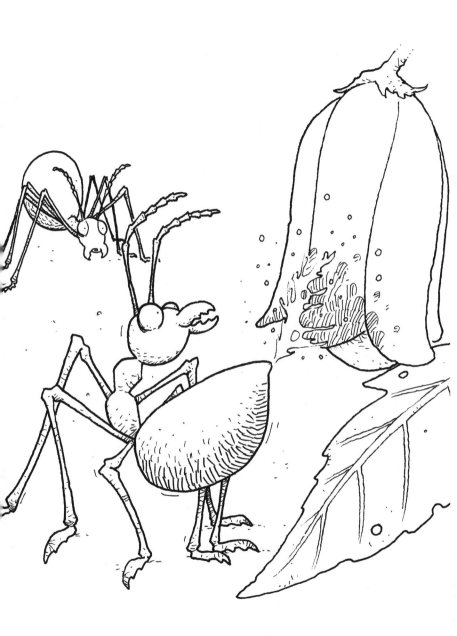

"This is serious, though," said Josh. "Of all the things we've been so far, this is the tiniest. We're going to get eaten or squashed at any moment. We have to get back to being human again."

"Well," said Danny. "We know S.W.I.T.C.H. spray is temporary. We just need a safe place to hide until we change back again. Or should we try to get to Petty?"

"She'll never see us!" said Josh. "She could hardly see us when we were grasshoppers." He looked around. "I think we're down in the sidewalk by the greenhouse. There's tons of ants around there. They are always building those little crumbly nests."

"We should find them!" said Danny. "There's safety in numbers!" He ran up the wall and straight over the top. Josh raced after him. He wondered how long they'd take to find a real ant!

As he popped his head up over the crumbly gray edge of the sidewalk, he stopped wondering. It was like stepping onto the highway at rush hour. There, in a huge, endless, nonstop line, rushing across the sidewalk, were hundreds of ants.

And he had no idea which one was Danny.

Pop

"DANNY! DANNY!" bawled Josh. His feelers and his scent-squirting gear were going nuts. "WHERE ARE YOU?"

A dark brown head turned to look at him, its feelers waving with interest. And then another one. And another one. At least forty ants in the long line were now peering back at him. "On," said the nearest one.

"You what?" said Josh.

"On," the ant repeated. She rather impatiently waved her feelers back in the direction that the ant line was traveling. "Must feed young."

"Look—yes—of course," said Josh scuttling up next to the ant. "But I'm trying to find my brother!"

The ant gave him a blank look. "I mean—sister," gulped Josh. The ant ignored him and just walked on.

"Another ant—like me," said Josh, desperately, walking alongside her. "We're not from here . . ."

The ant turned to stare at him. "Not from us?" she said. "Not?"

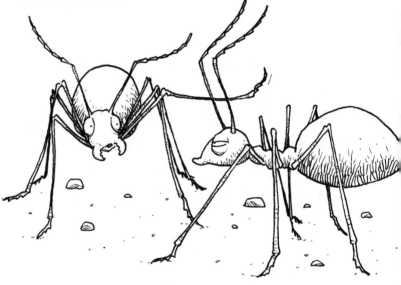

Josh suddenly remembered something from one of his insect books. Something important. Ants did not like ants from different colonies. Not at all. It was murder if someone came to visit. Really. Murder. If this colony found out that he and Danny were strangers, they'd pull them to pieces.

"Yes—yes—of course, from us!" Josh gabbled. "We're all family here!" He heard himself give a nervous titter. He was quite certain that no normal ant ever tittered. He must get a grip. He stepped away and let the suspicious ant walk on. Fortunately he must smell OK, because she didn't raise the alarm. She just muttered: "On. Must feed young."

"DANNEEEE!" wailed Josh. He stared around him at the huge alien world their backyard had become. Its rock garden was now looming up like Mount Everest, small shrubs now towered over him like giant redwood trees, and the sidewalk was as wide as a football field. "Where are you?"

"JOSH! JOSH!" hissed an excited voice above him. Josh stared up and saw Danny hanging down from the thick green trunk of a bush. "JOSH, GET UP HERE! IT'S AMAZING!"

"What is?" spluttered Josh. Danny just hung down on his back four legs and grabbed Josh with his jaws and forelegs and swung him up onto the slanting green stalk alongside him. "Will you stop that?" complained Josh. "I'm not a football!"

"No, but you're ever so easy to carry!" said Danny. "I'm superstrong. I am!"

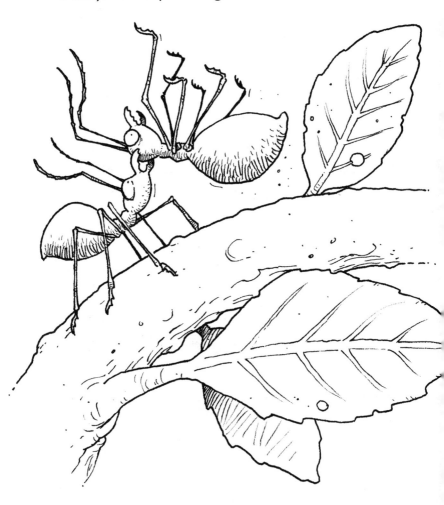

"Yep," said Josh. "Ants are. They can carry up to fifty times their own weight." He grabbed hold of Danny now, with his own jaws and forelegs. He waved his brother easily up in the air to make his point. Two or three other ants traveled past them along the green stalk. None of them paid any attention to Josh and Danny's circus act.

"All right, all right!" muttered Danny. "Put me down. And now come and see this!" He jumped back onto the green stalk. It was spongy and slightly sticky under their feet, and ran up it.

Josh could smell something wonderful. It reminded him of the smell at a fair—cotton candy! Hot, sweet, cotton candy! He hurried after Danny.

Danny had slowed down. He seemed to be cuddling something small, green, and slightly see-through. "It's so sweet!" crooned Danny, just like a girl with a kitten.

Josh sighed. They were girls, he kept remembering.

"Looook! So sweeeet!" went on Danny. He

turned the little green creature so it could look
up at Josh with its round black eyes. It waved
its small feelers in a friendly way. Danny stroked
its back with his own antennae. Then there was
a small pop, and a shiny blob of sticky stuff
suddenly oozed out of the little creature's back
end. Danny made a slurping noise, and the blob
disappeared.

"Try it!" he gurgled. "It's just like golden syrup!
Really sweet!"

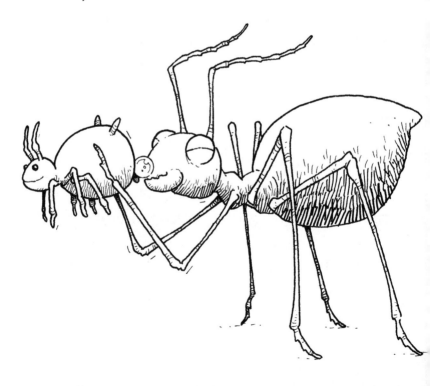

Josh gave a hoot of laughter. "Danny! You're eating aphid poo!"

"I know! I know!" gasped Danny. "How disgusting is that? But they were all at it." He nodded to the other ants around them. They were also stroking and cuddling the little green aphids and eating the substance that squished out of them.

"And it smelled so good. I just had to try it. And you know, they are cute!" His little aphid gazed up at him and made a gentle burbling noise.

"I think they call it honeydew," said Josh, picking up an aphid of his own now. This one also burbled gently and gazed up at him. "They drink the sugary stuff out of the plant and poo it out again. It's just like a big drop of candy. Ants love it."

He gave the aphid a friendly pat and a rub. Pop! Out came a shiny ball of syrupy goo. It did smell fantastic. Josh slurped it up and put the aphid down again. He felt sugar energy rush through him. "Look, this is all very nice," he said, with a hiccup. "But we've still got to find somewhere safe to hide until the S.W.I.T.C.H. spray wears off. Come on—let's get into the sandbox and hide there. There won't be many bugs in it because Mom changed the sand just this morning. It should be quite safe. We can hide under a few chunks of sand, out of the view of predators, until we go back to being human."

"OK, I've had enough aphid poo now, anyway. Bye-bye, Alfie!" Danny put the little green creature back onto the stalk. They scrambled back down, passing several other ants climbing up. "They don't say much, do they?" said Danny.

"No. Not big talkers," said Josh. "Some experts say they're just like one big living thing with millions of parts, working together. So they all think and say the same thing."

"What—like that?" asked Danny, as they rejoined the long ant highway and heard the endless chant. "On. Must feed young. On. Must feed young. On . . ."

"Yeah," said Josh. "Like that. It's like they've got no will of their own." He found himself falling into step with the long line of marching insects. Danny stepped in behind him.

"On. Must feed young," said Danny, in the same robotic sort of voice as the others.

"We'll travel with them for a while," said Josh. "It's safer—but we can go off when we get to the end of the sidewalk and head for the sandbox."

"On," said Danny.

"All right?" said Josh.

"Must feed young," said Danny.

"OK, very funny!" Josh glanced over his shiny shoulder. He saw that Danny was marching exactly in time with the ants around him. "Over to the sandbox as soon as we can, right?"

"Must feed young," said Danny.

"Stop messing around! This is serious!" squawked Josh.

"On," said Danny.

Josh wanted to give his brother a telling off. But the words didn't come out right. "On," he said, turning his head back toward the front and marching in step with all the others. "Must feed young."

"Must feed young," agreed Danny.

"Must feed young," said the other 1,124 ants sharing their journey.

Happy Ant Day

"YOU'RE JUST JERKS! BOTH OF YOU!" shouted
Tarquin. He shook the spray bottle and stamped
his foot. "COME OUT OF HIDING! I'LL TELL
YOUR MOM! I WILL."

Still there was no movement or sound around
the yard. Tarquin had already looked behind or
under everything he could see. There was no sign
of Josh or Danny. He knew they were playing a
trick on him. Maybe they'd gone next door into
that old lady's garden. They'd dropped their water
pistols on the ground, so at least they weren't
planning another ambush. Maybe they'd got
something else to throw or squirt at him and were
just waiting for him to climb up and put his head
over the wooden fence.

"WELL, I'M NOT PLAYING, ANYMORE!"

yelled Tarquin. He turned and stomped back along the sidewalk. The old lady from next door was walking back down it on her side of the wall. As she passed him, she gave a shout, reached over the wall, and scooped the spray bottle out of his hand.

"What are you doing with my bottle?" she demanded.

"Nothing!" snapped Tarquin. "Not anymore! I only got the chance to give them both one squirt before they ran away and hid."

Petty Potts grabbed him by the ear. "You did what?"

"Owww! I told you! I just squirted at them once. What's the fuss? It was only a bit of water."

Petty glared at him angrily and said, "It was my bit of water, and you had no business stealing it!"

"Well, how was I to know?" whined Tarquin. She let him go, looking very worried.

"They disappeared, you say?"

"Yes, they must have run off and hid while I was wiping water out of my eyes."

"Oh dear. Oh dear, oh dear, oh dear," said Petty. She bit her lip.

"Batty old trout," muttered Tarquin. He made his escape and ran back around through the front door.

Inside the house, Piddle the dog heard him coming. He scrabbled into the front room and

behind the sofa with another whine. Tarquin
stamped up the stairs and went to find something
to play with in Josh and Danny's room. There
wasn't much he liked. He wasn't into all those
stupid Legos or those silly battling card games.
But he picked up the magnifying glass and
decided to take it into the yard. The sun was
shining, and he was in the mood for a particularly
nasty game.

It was warm in the ants' nest and filled with
"home" and "family" smells. These smells
instructed the family to do all kinds of things.
Feed the young, mend broken walls, look after
the queen, go out and forage for food, and so on.
Once they were in the nest, Danny and Josh got
a bit confused. The ants weren't all chanting the
same thing anymore. There were lots of different
chants and instructions going on.

Josh turned around and stared at Danny.
He stood there, waggling his feelers for a few
seconds, while ants streamed past him in all
directions. He finally said, "Danny! What are we
doing here? Why did we follow the others in?"

"I don't know," said Danny with a shrug. He stared around at the complicated brown-walled tunnels that led off at every angle. Knotty roots dangled here and there and seemed to hold all the chunks of soil and grit together. "It seemed like a good idea at the time."

"Well, it's not a good idea now!" said Josh. He looked around at the endless traffic of super-busy ants. Even though there were huge numbers

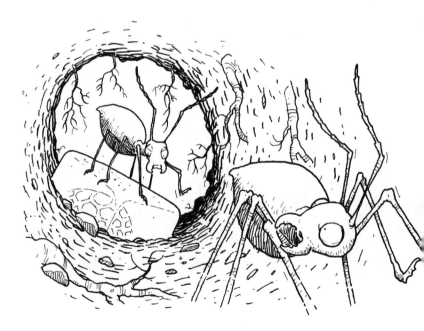

of them, they never seemed to bump into one another. Not even the ones walking upside down on the ceiling. "We've got to get out of here and get to the sandbox!" He began to work his way back up the tunnel. "Come on! We can't stay here. If all that chanting starts again, we might find ourselves feeding larvae forever!"

"Well, just until the S.W.I.T.C.H. spray wears off and we suddenly burst through the nest, back to our usual size!" said Danny.

"Danny, we're down underneath the sidewalk! If we suddenly shoot up to full size, we'll crack our heads open!" shuddered Josh. "Come on—we can't stay here a minute longer!"

Danny hurried after his brother. Josh was running over a shiny piece of glass, wrapped in winding grass roots. The glass sparkled in the narrow shaft of light that fed down from the nest entrance. Josh stopped.

Danny cannoned into him. "COME ON, JOSH! YOU SAID WE'VE GOT TO GET OUT FAST!"

"Yes, but . . ." Josh was peering down at the glass that glimmered up between the roots.

"This . . . this is . . ." He thought he could make out a tiny turtle peering up at him. It was stirring up a memory. What about? He shook his head and scurried after Danny. Clearly all the ant chanting was driving him a bit crazy. What would a tiny turtle be doing in an ants' nest?

They found their way out by following the scent of the air above them. But as soon as they reached the nest exit, Danny started to look dazed.

The "ON. MUST FEED YOUNG" chant was so loud out here. "DANNY! DON'T LISTEN!" yelled Josh. His brother started to turn and rejoin the marching ants. "DANNY! SING! SING WITH ME!"

Danny looked back at his brother, and Josh started singing.

> Happy ant day to you!
> Happy ant day to you!

Danny joined in.

> Happy ant day, dear anty.
> Have some more aphid poo!

"YES—AGAIN!" shouted Josh. By the time they'd sung it through three times, they were away from the long line of chanting ants. They went over a bridge of hairy green moss to the next slab of sidewalk and ran toward the sandbox.

For a few seconds, it seemed as if they were clear. Then there was a thundering sensation, and a stampede almost swept them off their feet. This ant line was much less ordered, and the chanting was wild and excited. "Sweet! Sweet! Sweet! Sweet!" Danny and Josh found themselves carried along, toward something that filled the air with an even more sugary smell than the aphids.

"LOOK!" gasped Josh.

A wide lake lay before them. It gleamed red in the sun and sent out the tantalizing smell. "What is it?" murmured Danny.

"Whatever it is, it's sweet!" said Josh. All around him the ants were saying the same, "Sweet! Sweet! Sweet! Sweet!" And they were all clustering around the edges and gleefully drinking from it. Across the middle of the lake, Josh could make out a very long wooden walkway. Some of the ants were scurrying along it to get to the rosy syrup beneath it. It was tipping sideways rather dangerously. Josh suddenly declared, "I know what it is! I know!"

"What?" said Danny. "It smells amazing. Shall we have some?"

"No, it's too dangerous," said Josh. "Look!" And he waved his feelers toward two or three ants that had become trapped in the gloopy red liquid. They were struggling hopelessly. "They're never getting out of it. You've killed them."

"Me? What are you saying?"

"It's your fault. You left half of your Popsicle there on the sidewalk this morning. You ate the top part and then left the strawberry part still on the stick. So it's melted, and now it's a sugar lake feeding frenzy. Ants will drown in it! They always do . . ."

Danny gulped. "But they seemed so sensible before—so organized. Now they're going bonkers!"

He was right. Hundreds of ants were now charging to the lake. It looked like some kind of wild rock festival going on. They clambered over one another and shoved one another aside to get to the front.

"Sugar. Drives them nuts," sighed Josh. "Especially in the summer. You want to meet a few thousand ants? Just drop a Popsicle on the ground and wait. Crowds of spaced-out sugar zombies that can't think straight. It's nearly as bad as our last birthday party."

Danny felt bad. "Come on," he said, fighting his way back through the crowds of sugar-crazed ants. "We've got to get to the sandbox."

"We're nearly at the edge of the sidewalk," yelled Josh. "We just have to go past those old bricks that Dad put there." The angle of red bricks had been cemented to the corner of the slab when Dad decided to make a barbecue. He hadn't done any more yet, so the bricks weren't very high. Unless you happened to be an ant. Now they loomed up like great tower blocks.

"Could go over them," said Danny, as they drew closer. "We can run up walls, no problem."

"No, might get seen by a bird," warned Josh. At least against the speckled gray of the sidewalk they didn't stand out that much. But they would on red brick. "Better go around."

"OK, but we—" Danny stopped because Josh had stopped. Josh was standing still and waving his feelers in the air. There was a big, rumbly, crackly feeling coming in through his antennae. Something big, rumbly, crackly . . . and hot. Very hot. An incredibly bright light flashed in their eyes.

"WHAT'S THAT?" shouted Danny. "Josh— what is it?"

Josh stared back at Danny. His feelers quivered. "I don't like this. I don't like this at all . . ."

Fries, Anyone?

"Smell it!" whispered Josh. He sent great big waves of fear out through his scent-squirting gear. "It smells . . . like . . . burning."

There was another bright flash, and then they saw it. Something truly terrifying. A huge, brilliant, blindingly white pillar of fire. It was hitting the edge of the sidewalk on the far side. They could sense panic among the ant colony they had just run away from. The terrible rumbling and burning was getting louder and stronger. Josh and Danny could see the pillar of fire moving from left to right, tilting at an angle, like a tornado, but not so shaky. Little pops and bursts of flame kept going off under it. Danny didn't want to think about what they were.

"What is it?" gasped Josh. "What could be

making that happen? It's vaporizing everything in its path!"

Danny gulped and squinted up. Above them—high, high up in the sky, was a round glow, like the sun. Shooting out from the round glow was the pillar of fire. A dim shape loomed up somewhere beyond it. "OH NO!" shrieked Danny. "I know what it is! I know what it is! Josh! Don't stand there looking! RUN! WE'VE GOT TO RUN BEFORE HE SEES US!"

"He?" spluttered Josh. He legged it along behind Danny as fast as he could. "Who's he?"

"It's Tarquin!" shouted back Danny.

"Tarquin? With a death ray? Who made him a god?"

"YOU did!" Danny reached the bottom of the redbrick tower. "When you let him pick up your magnifying glass! If he likes picking legs off things, I bet he's into frying things too. He's making the sun shine through the glass like a laser and frying everything that moves!"

"Oh no!" wailed Josh. He spun around as he reached his brother and took in the terrible sight behind them. "It's coming this way! He must have seen us!"

The crackling, smoking, white-hot beam wandered off to the left for a second, exploding something that looked like a poor little beetle. Then it moved relentlessly toward the brick wall corner that Josh and Danny were now backed into.

"Quick—we've got to run around the bricks and hide!" squeaked Josh.

"No—up and over! It's quicker!" yelled Danny. "I don't care about the birds! We've got a death ray to worry about."

He scrambled up the wall as fast as his three pairs of legs could carry him. Josh hurried up alongside him. Glancing backward, he could see it was hopeless. The death ray was speeding across the slab, heading straight for them. Any second now, one of them would be toast. And then the other.

"If he gets me first, just keep running!" gasped Danny. He was also looking back over his shoulder. But the beam, as it got closer, was big enough to get them both. It swept up the wall, sending up a plume of hot, fine, redbrick dust. "Oh no—we're done for," wailed Danny. He scrunched up into a ball on the edge of the brick. "Bye-bye, Josh. You've been a great brother . . . for a freaky little bug geek."

Josh scrunched up into a ball as well. "Bye, Danny," he gulped, sadly. "You too . . . for a skateboard nut."

The Heat Is On/Off/On

THWACK!

"You nasty little tick!" Petty Potts slammed her net down over Tarquin's head. "Are you really setting fire to innocent insects?"

Tarquin squawked with rage. He dropped the magnifying glass onto the sidewalk and struggled to get the net off his head. "Get off! Get it off me, you horrid old woman! My mother will have the police on to you, I tell you."

"Murderer," muttered Petty. She kept the net firmly in place and waved a small flashlightlike device at the sidewalk.

"They're only ants!"

Petty gulped. It was ants she was looking for. Her S.W.I.T.C.H.ee detector was bleeping off the scale. Now she was certain that Josh and

Danny had been S.W.I.T.C.H.ed—and very likely barbecued. That would be a little awkward. Shoving Tarquin out of the way, she knelt to peer at the bricks where the loathsome child had been directing the magnifying glass. She could just about make out two of the little creatures. They were cowering close together on the top edge. Could that be Josh and Danny? Could it? If so, they should be about to return to their proper shape any moment now, judging by her calculations. She turned off the S.W.I.T.C.H.ee detector and checked her watch.

"GET THIS OFF ME!" shouted Tarquin again. He was still struggling pathetically with the net.

Petty flicked it off the boy. "Go—shoo, you repulsive little gargoyle!" she told him. Tarquin ran away, much to her relief. Now, were those two really Josh and Danny? Or was that just wishful thinking?

"Danny!" whispered Josh, unscrunching a little. A cloud of hot brick dust swirled around him, stinging his eyes. "Danny? Are you there?"

Danny looked out from his own scrunch and waggled his feelers shakily. "Yes. I'm here. What happened?"

"It's gone! The death ray—it's gone!"

They stared all around them. There was no sign of the death ray.

"Phew-hoo!" hooted Danny, running over to Josh and doing a high five with him, with one feeler. "We're not little piles of anty ash!"

"It's gone," sighed Josh. "We're safe."

"Josh—Danny—is that you?" whispered Petty, screwing up her eyes and trying to see. Oh, here was the magnifying glass. That would help.

Considering she was a genius, Petty had occasional moments of being very, very stupid. This was one now. She picked up the glass and held it over the two ants.

"AAAAAAAAAAAAAAAAAAAAHHHHH!" screamed Josh and Danny as a blast of white heat suddenly hit them.

Oops

Petty was just beginning to realize that she was in fact killing the little ants she was hoping to help. Then she was walloped in the face.

It was Danny who bashed her glasses sideways and nearly flattened her nose. To be fair, he was just about to perish in a sea of flame when he abruptly returned to human form. So you couldn't blame him for lashing out a bit. The sea of flame did cause a slight mark on his knee, he later discovered.

Josh didn't smack anyone in the face. He just sprawled into the sandbox. The blaze that had started on his right eyebrow was instantly put out.

"Oh! Oh! Oh! What a relief!" gasped Petty, fanning her face and swaying on her knees.

"Give me that!" Danny grabbed the magnifying glass. He shoved it safely into his pants pocket.

"It wasn't me trying to incinerate you!" protested Petty. "I was just trying to find you and save you. Sorry it got a bit hot, though. I forgot about that magnified sunlight business for a few seconds there. No—the one who was trying to kill you was that ghastly child from around the corner."

"What—*that* ghastly child?" said Josh standing up. Tarquin came back into the garden holding on to their mom's hand. He was looking wounded and sulky.

"Now, now, boys—Tarquin says you won't play with him," said their mom. "Oh, hello, Miss Potts."

"Hello, dear," said Petty standing up. "Just looking at insects with your sons. I'm sure Tarquin is very welcome to join in. I'm off now—see you all later."

And she hurried out of the garden with her S.W.I.T.C.H.ee detector, whistling with relief.

"No, he's not welcome," said Josh. "He just tried to kill us."

Mom looked astonished. "Really, boys, don't be so silly! What possible harm could little Tarquin do?" Little Tarquin smirked at them from under her arm.

"Well, if he'd got the chance he'd have pulled our legs off," said Danny.

Mom laughed. "You boys! Really! Here—I've brought some Popsicles for you all." She gave them to Danny to hand out and went back into the house.

Danny grinned. He'd had an idea. He whispered to Josh as Tarquin ripped off his Popsicle wrapper and began slurping noisily. "Shall we?" said Danny, and Josh grinned back and nodded.

"Come on then," said Danny. "Let's sit here." He led Tarquin over to sit on the sidewalk. As they walked, Danny mashed his own Popsicle in one hand. He let it drip onto the ground.

They all sat down. Danny melted more Popsicle while Josh kept Tarquin talking. Soon the sweet little yellow blobs made a pathway from a crumbly bit of soil at the edge of the sidewalk. Right up to their visitor's pants legs and a little way inside. Then Danny shuffled closer to Tarquin. He patted him on the back a few times, in a friendly, sticky way.

Tarquin didn't notice the crazy sugar pop festival for quite a while. Not until it had gotten up across his jacket, scurried down inside his collar, and marched some way up his pants leg.

"Who was screeching?" asked Mom a few minutes later. She emerged from the house with Tarquin's mom.

"Is that my Tarquin, doing a little dance down along the garden?" said Tarquin's mom.

"Nothing to worry about," said Josh, with a happy smile.

"He's just got ants in his pants," said Danny.

Nest Quest

Tarquin had at last gone home with his mother, wearing a spare pair of Danny's shorts and crying loudly. Mom brought a cup of tea and some little cakes out to them in the garden.

"Just to say thanks," she said. She handed them the tray as they sat on the garden bench. "For trying. He's an annoying boy. Gives you heartburn."

"You'll never know," mumbled Danny, through a mouthful of cake.

Josh picked up the pink-iced sponge cube and stared at it as Mom went back indoors.

"Well go on, then," said Danny. "You love French Fancies."

Josh raised his eyes up above the cake. He stared at Danny, a slow smile spreading over his face.

"Now I know what I saw in the ants' nest!" he breathed.

"Yes," said Danny. "Ants. A lot of them."

"Not just ants! I saw a tiny turtle too!"

"A tiny turtle too?" echoed Danny, wondering if Josh had decided to start making up funny songs. "A tiddly turtle too . . . having a piddly poo?" he ventured.

Josh sprang to his feet and slammed the cake down on the plate. "DANNY! I KNOW WHERE ANOTHER REPTOSWITCH CUBE IS!" And he began to run toward the sidewalk. "COME ON! Petty's going to get another of her missing cubes back today! That'll be four out of six. Maybe that will be enough to crack the reptile S.W.I.T.C.H. code. You never know!"

At the sidewalk, they peered down into the crumbly brown nests in the cracks. "I saw sparkly glass in the ants' nest tunnel, just before we ran back out," explained Josh. "And while I was looking into it, I saw a turtle looking back up at me! It couldn't have been a real turtle. Not in an ants' nest. It must be a hologram! A hologram in another one of Petty's missing cubes!"

He poked his fingers down into the nest, scattering dozens of panicked ants. "Here! This is where we came out, I'm sure. Danny, help me get the slab up!"

"What are you two doing?" called Mom, looking out of the kitchen window.

"Just looking at an ants' nest," called back Danny.

"Oh, that reminds me," said Mom. She disappeared back through the window.

The slab was heavy, but between them, Josh and Danny managed to pry the edge up and lift it away. Underneath, a secret world was revealed. A flat gray plain of soil and grit and roots, with centipedes and woodlice fleeing across it as the daylight struck them. A complicated network of passages wriggled across the surface, and scores of ants were running along them in a frenzy.

Josh and Danny knew that the tunnels went much deeper than this. "How far down was the cube, then?" asked Danny.

"Can't be that deep—maybe ten inches . . . ?" guessed Josh. "Look—there's the main entrance."

He pointed to a larger hole through which a long chain of ants was hurrying.

A shadow fell across them. Josh and Danny glanced up, and there stood Mom. She was holding a glinting deadly weapon in her hand. A kettle.

Steam rose from its spout in menacing curls.

"Look out," said Mom. "I've been meaning to do this all week. We've got far too many ants."

"NOOOOOOO!!" screamed Josh and Danny, both together.

Mom blinked. She had expected Josh to protest a bit—but Danny? He didn't even like creepy-crawlies! She'd poured boiling water on nests before, and he'd never batted an eyelid!

"You can't!" cried Josh. "It's cruel! You'll wipe out an entire family and all their babies."

"DON'T DO IT, MOM!" begged Danny.

Mom stepped back, shrugging. One steaming splash of water hit the nest. It left a crater of hot mud. "All right! All right!" she said. "But don't blame me if you get ants in your pants like Tarquin!"

"We won't mind!" said Danny.

At last, Mom went away. They breathed a huge sigh of relief. It was one thing to wipe out a nest of ants when you'd only just noticed them by your toes. Quite another thing when you'd met them all and been in their house.

"OK, I'll be careful," said Josh. He prodded his fingers gently and slowly down through the main entrance. After only a few seconds, as the crumbly earth gave way, he felt a cold, hard angle of glass. In a moment he had seized it and wiggled it out of the embrace of the grass roots.

He knelt back and held it up to the light. One perfect glass cube, with a tiny, delicate hologram of a turtle inside it. He and Danny stared at each other, grinning excitedly. Then they leapt to their feet and tore around the house. Seconds later, they were hammering on Petty's front door.

Petty Potts pulled them into her hallway and slammed the door. Then she took the cube from Josh's hand and stared at it, thrilled.

"Where was it?" she whispered.

"In an ants' nest in our yard," said Josh. "We would never have found it if we hadn't been turned into ants ourselves."

"Oh yes," said Danny, suddenly remembering.

"What were you thinking of, giving S.W.I.T.C.H. spray to Tarquin?"

"I didn't give it to him, you donkey!" said Petty. She was still smiling mistily into the cube. "He just grabbed it when I left it on the wall for ten seconds."

"You've got to be more careful," said Josh.

"I am careful," insisted Petty. "And anyway, if you hadn't been turned into ants, we would never have got this back!"

They didn't bother to go on arguing because she was too entranced by the cube to pay any attention. She walked into the kitchen and got two boxes down from a high shelf. One was red velvet, and one was green velvet. The red one, as she opened it, revealed a set of six perfect glass cubes. The BUGSWITCH cubes. Their six holograms contained the six parts of the code for making BUGSWITCH spray.

Now Petty opened the green box. In this lay three cubes and three empty dents. Petty pressed the fourth cube into its dent and sighed happily.

"Just two more to find!" she murmured. "Two more and the REPTOSWITCH code will be mine again! Mine! MINE!"

She glanced at Josh and Danny and coughed. "I mean . . . ours." She smiled at them. "And when it's complete, you two will be the first humans on Earth to know how it feels to be a reptile! An alligator! A giant lizard! A python! Whatever you want! I will be able to make the spray . . ."

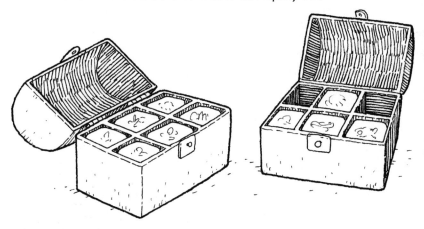

"Will it make us rich?" wondered Danny. Danny liked money.

"Of course," said Petty. "But more importantly, it will make us the most famous scientists in the world!"

A shadow moved outside Petty's kitchen window. She flinched and went to stare outside. "Did you see that?" she whispered.

"What? It was probably just a cat," said Josh.

Petty turned away from the window and stared at them both. "You ought to know..." she said, her eyes glittering, "...that the closer we get to finding the REPTOSWITCH code, the more dangerous it could get."

Danny blinked. "Look, we've been nearly eaten by a centipede and then burnt alive by a magnifying glass today. I think we know how dangerous it gets."

"No, I mean . . . we're probably being watched."
Petty flicked a glance back over her shoulder. "By
them . . ."

"Them?" said Josh.

"They have a file on me," said Petty. "I might
have been expelled from the government's secret
laboratories, but they've always been watching
me. The mailman, the milkman, the lady who
delivers fish . . . any one of them could be a
government spy working for Victor Crouch.
He might have burnt my memory out, but he'll
always have someone on the lookout, just in case.
Watching and waiting. Waiting for a sign that my
work goes on! He failed to steal it properly before.
The he burnt out my memory before he realized
his stupid mistake—that the notes he stole from
me were all faked. He will always wonder if it's
possible for me to start again. And just in case, he
will always have someone watching. . . ."

"O . . . K," said Josh. "Time for us to go home
now. Byeeeee."

"I tell you! They're like ants! They're
everywhere!" insisted Petty, snapping the velvet

boxes shut. "Be on your guard! Tell me if you see anything suspicious! Anything at all . . ."

"She's bonkers," said Danny. Petty closed her front door, and they walked down the front garden path. "Every bonkers person thinks the government is spying on them."

"Yep," said Josh.

Across the road, the man emptying the mailbox finished filling up his sack. Then, when nobody seemed to be looking, he took out a pair of binoculars and trained them on Petty Potts's house . . .

Top Secret!

For Petty Potts's Eyes Only!!

SUBJECT: FOUR PARTS OF THE CODE NOW FOUND

Whoever would have thought it? Danny and Josh got turned into ants today, quite by mistake. Of course, it was useful for my research. I will get them to tell me the details tomorrow.

But MUCH more importantly, while they were ants, they went into a nest in their yard and found the fourth REPTOSWITCH cube!!! I am now two-thirds of the way back to getting the reptile morphing code!!!

I always knew that I would have hidden the cubes close to home. But I may never remember exactly where. I just hope that the final two are discovered soon. Before one of Victor Crouch's spies gets wind of how Josh and Danny are helping.

$$\frac{4 \times \pi^2}{0S-7^*} \searrow \frac{\boxed{P_2}}{0.8} \times \frac{\sqrt{6^2 \, 0/9}}{9.15^\circ_F} = \frac{4.198}{\frac{4.197}{(548)}}$$

I dreamed of Crouch last night. He was staring at me and waving his spiky, black little finger. I was throwing lizards at him, but he didn't look shocked. Well, a man with no eyebrows can't really look shocked.

But that's not important. The important thing is my genius move to get Josh and Danny on board is still working out well. After all, who is ever going to believe that two eight-year-olds are helping me on the project?

But I have had to warn them about the spies. I don't think they believed me. I might have to show them some evidence of my life before, when I worked with Victor in the government's secret underground labs. And I should probably show them his photograph. They need to be on their guard now.

They may only be children, but that wouldn't stop Victor if he ever found out what they knew. That wouldn't stop him at all. . . .

REMEMBER →

$$\frac{60}{\frac{OUP}{\pi}} \rightarrow \cancel{\cancel{\phi}} \rightarrow \frac{1}{2}st^2$$

Recommended Reading

BOOKS
Want to brush up on your bug knowledge? Here's a list of books dedicated to creepy-crawlies.

Glaser, Linda. *Not a Buzz to Be Found.* Minneapolis: Millbrook Press, 2012.

Heos, Bridget. *What to Expect When You're Expecting Larvae: A Guide for Insect Parents (and Curious Kids).* Minneapolis: Millbrook Press, 2011.

Markle, Sandra. Insect World series. Minneapolis: Lerner Publications, 2008.

WEBSITES
Find out more about nature and wildlife using the websites below.

BioKids
http://www.biokids.umich.edu/critters/
The University of Michigan's Critter Catalog has

a ton of pictures of different kinds of bugs and information on where they live, how they behave, and their predators.

National Geographic Kids
http://video.nationalgeographic.com/video/kids
/animals-pets-kids/bugs-kids
Go to this fun website to watch clips from National Geographic about all sorts of creepy-crawlies.

U.S. Fish & Wildlife Service
http://www.fws.gov/letsgooutside/kids.html
This website has lots of activities for when you're outside playing and looking for wildlife.

CHECK OUT ALL OF THE

#1 Spider Stampede

Eight-year-olds Josh and Danny discover that their neighbor Miss Potts has a secret formula that can change people into bugs. Soon enough, they find themselves with six extra legs. Can the boys survive in the world as spiders long enough to make it home in time for dinner?

#2 Fly Frenzy

Danny and Josh are avoiding their neighbor because she "accidentally" turned them into bugs. But when their mom's garden is ruined the day before a big competition, the twins turn into bluebottle houseflies to discover the culprits. Will they find who's responsible before it's too late?

#3 Grasshopper Glitch

Danny and Josh are having a normal day at school . . . until they turn into grasshoppers in the middle of class! Can they avoid being eaten during their whirlwind search to find the antidote? And will they be able to change back before getting a week of detention?

 **TITLES!**

#4 Ant Attack

Danny and Josh are being forced to play with Tarquin, the most annoying boy in the neighborhood. But things get dangerous when the twins accidentally turn into ants and discover that Tarquin kills bugs for fun.... Can they find a safe place to hide until they turn human again?

#5 Crane Fly Crash

When Petty Potts leaves town, she puts Danny and Josh in charge of some of her S.W.I.T.C.H. spray. Unfortunately, their sister, Jenny, mistakes it for hair spray and ends up as a crane fly. Now it's up to the twins to keep Jenny from being eaten alive.

#6 Beetle Blast

Danny is forced to go with his brother, Josh, to his nature group, but neither of them thought they would turn into the nature they were studying! Both brothers become beetles just in time to learn about pond dipping ... from the bug's perspective. Can they avoid getting caught by the other kids?

About the Author

Ali Sparkes grew up in the woods of Hampshire, England. Actually, strictly speaking, she grew up in a house in Hampshire. The woods were great but lacked basic facilities like sofas and a well-stocked fridge. Nevertheless, the woods were where she and her friends spent much of their time, and so Ali grew up with a deep and abiding love of wildlife. If you ever see Ali with a large garden spider on her shoulder, she will most likely be screeching, "AAAARRRGHGETITOFFME!"

Ali lives in Southampton with her husband and sons. She would never kill a creepy-crawly of any kind. They are more scared of her than she is of them. (Creepy-crawlies, not her husband and sons.)

About the Illustrator

Ross Collins's more than eighty picture books and books for young readers have appeared in print around the world. He lives in Scotland and, in his spare time, enjoys leaning backward precariously in his chair.